MW01148578

This book is dedicated to all the courageous rescued animals. They've simply experienced more life than other animals. They are the souls with tales to tell and stories to write about finding their adoptive forever homes.

www.mascotbooks.com

Angel's Forever Home

©2019 Rita Gigante, Bobbie Sterchele-Gigante, and Donna McDine. All Rights Reserved. No part of this publication may be reproduced, stored in a retrieval system or transmitted in any form by any means electronic, mechanical, or photocopying, recording or otherwise without the permission of the author.

For more information, please contact:
Mascot Books
620 Herndon Parkway, Suite 320
Herndon, VA 20170
info@mascotbooks.com

Library of Congress Control Number: 2018910288

CPSIA Code: PRT1118A
ISBN-13: 978-1-64307-121-3

Printed in the United States

Angel's
Forever Home

Rita Gigante
Bobbie Sterchele-Gigante
Co-written by Donna McDine
Illustrated by Renie De Mase

After being rescued
from a Chilean earthquake by
American dog rescuer Jill, Angel
found himself on a journey to the USA.
The journey was long, but it didn't
take Angel long to settle in at Jill's
house. He lay happily on the grass in
the front garden as Jill rubbed his belly.
"Your leg needs serious help," said
Jill. "And we must also find you a good
forever home."

Woo-ah! I thought this WAS my forever home? thought Angel. He stopped thumping his tail and stared sadly at Jill.

"Don't worry, Angel, I've advertised. I'll carefully check out everyone who applies. You'll be happy, I promise."

Angel thought about a forever home while Jill rubbed his belly again and the wind chimes sang their song. *Jill did save me,* he thought. *I should trust her to find me a good forever home.*

One day, a man and woman came to the gate. "Do you have a dog for us to adopt?" they asked.

Will these be my new people? thought Angel. Excited, he struggled to stand up and moved toward the gate.

"What happened to him?" the woman asked. The man frowned.

"I rescued Angel from the aftermath of the Chilean earthquake," said Jill. "His leg was badly hurt during the quake. I want to find him a good home."

"We'd like to take him," said the man, "but we can't afford expensive veterinarian fees. Sorry."

The couple walked away.

Angel leaned against Jill. *Will anyone ever love me enough to take me home?* he wondered.

"Don't worry, Angel. Someone special will come along," said Jill. She gave Angel a gentle pat. "A kind person who will have your leg fixed and will play with you."

Play with me? Angel's ears pricked up.

Jill laughed. "That's right, play. But for now it's time for lunch."

After lunch, Angel sat outside in the warmth of the sun. *In this spot I get to keep an eye on the gate,* he thought.

A sudden breeze rushed through the wind chimes. They sounded louder than before. *Bong. Bong.*

A lone woman stood at the gate.

Angel raised his head. *Is this the special person Jill told me about?*

Jill went to the gate and asked, "You're here to meet Angel, right?"

"Yes, I am," said the woman, shaking Jill's hand.

Angel's stomach felt funny. A good funny. Not a nervous funny like he was going to throw up. *Let me just wait right here*, Angel thought. *If she sees my hurt leg, she might leave too.*

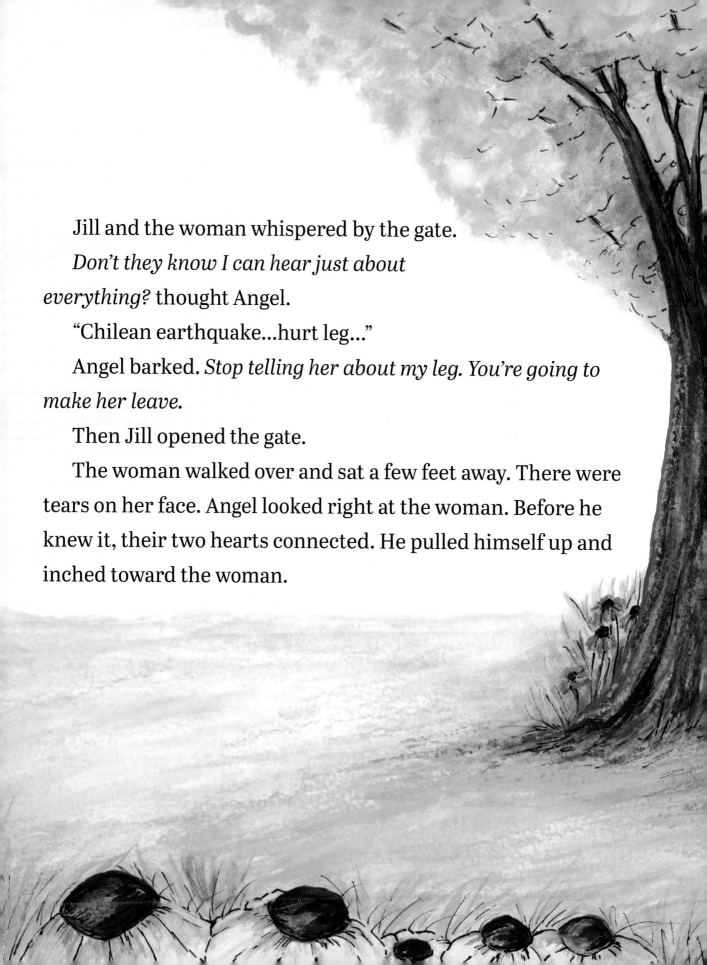

Jill and the woman whispered by the gate.

Don't they know I can hear just about everything? thought Angel.

"Chilean earthquake…hurt leg…"

Angel barked. *Stop telling her about my leg. You're going to make her leave.*

Then Jill opened the gate.

The woman walked over and sat a few feet away. There were tears on her face. Angel looked right at the woman. Before he knew it, their two hearts connected. He pulled himself up and inched toward the woman.

Please don't leave. I'm so much more than a hurt leg.
The woman held out her hands as Angel crept closer.
She's the one—I know it. Angel licked her fingers.

"Angel, this is Rita. She wants to offer you a safe, forever home," said Jill.

Angel rested his head on Rita's lap. As much as he loved the cool grass, her lap was so much better.

When are we going home? he thought as he nestled his head deeper.

Rita scratched Angel's jaw and whispered in his ear, "Home soon, Angel. Very soon."

Her warmth filled his heart.

Rita gave him a gentle hug and said, "My love, I need to go for now. I must speak with someone else, but I will return for you very soon."

Angel's joy grew as high as a rainbow. *Oh yes, I can wait.*

Two sunsets and two sunrises later, Angel's wait came to an end.

The gate swung open. Angel's tail wagged at super speed. *You're back! You're back!*

"I've brought a friend I thought you'd like to meet," said Rita as she scratched behind Angel's ear.

A friend? thought Angel.

A woman with pretty, dark eyes knelt beside him. "So nice to meet you. My name is Bobbie."

Angel stretched out on his side as far as he could to show Bobbie his belly. Bobbie knew just what to do. She scratched it right away.

This feels so good. Don't stop. Angel's tail thumped.

"I knew you'd love Angel," said Rita, with a grin on her face. Then she turned to Jill and said, "We want to adopt him."

Oh YES! A forever home with two people to play with. Angel almost burst with happiness.

"Are you sure? His leg requires surgery. It'll be expensive," cautioned Jill.

"We'll have him checked out by our veterinarian tomorrow. He'll do what's needed to fix that leg," Bobbie said confidently.

After many licks of thanks for Jill, Angel went off with Bobbie and Rita.

Without a word to anyone, Rita knew the leg could not be saved. Her sense of knowing was confirmed by the vet the next morning.

"I'm sorry, but we can't fix his leg. It must be removed. Please don't worry, dogs do just fine on three legs. And he won't be in pain anymore," explained the vet.

Only three legs? Angel thought very hard. *But the NO PAIN bit sounds great.*

The next day, while Angel was in surgery Rita and Bobbie paced the waiting room.

After a long time, the vet appeared, smiling. "Angel's surgery went well. He's in recovery now."

"May we see him?" Rita asked.

"It's important Angel rests," the vet explained. "Come back tomorrow morning and you may take him home."

The next morning, Angel felt groggy. *My head feels like it's stuffed with feathers,* he thought.

Rita thanked the vet and carried him to their car. Rita held Angel while Bobbie drove home.

"Careful now," fussed Bobbie as Rita carried him inside and placed him on the bed.

Angel looked around him. *Home, at last.* He settled on the comfy bed, yawned, and took a nap.

Rita laughed. "He looks quite at home."

"He sure does," said Bobbie.

When Angel woke up he felt like exploring. He wiggled, and a sharp pain shot through him. *Yikes! I thought removing my leg removed the pain.* He whimpered softly.

Bobbie sat beside him. "You must give your stump time to heal. Then you can race around and explore."

Rita lay beside Angel and stared into his soulful eyes. "Shhh, be still Angel. You need to rest."

I want to explore, thought Angel, sniffing the air. *My super sense of smell tells me there's another critter close by—like me.*

"Please be patient," Rita said. "You'll meet Sara in a few days. I think you'll like her."

As the vet promised, within a few days the pain eased, and Angel was able to get around on his three good legs.

A few days later, Rita said, "You are now well enough to meet a new friend."

Finally! thought Angel. *I've been so bored.* He sniffed the air. *There's that smell again.*

Sure enough, Bobbie came into the room followed by a shaggy, brown dog. "Angel, meet Sara," said Bobbie. The quiet dog settled in alongside Angel.

Angel sniffed Sara from head to toe. All the while, Sara lay there perfectly still.

Angel rested his paw on Sara's belly and said to her, "You are in pain."

Sara replied, "A car hit me and broke my hip. I had surgery to repair it."

"A tree fell on me during an earthquake and I lost my leg," said Angel. "I guess we're both lucky to have a forever home with Rita and Bobbie."

"Look at the two of them," said Rita, smiling at Angel and Sara's instant connection.

Days turned into weeks. Angel's stump healed and Sara's strength returned. Along with Angel's healing, Sara gained a bit of her spunk back. With her newfound energy, Sara never wanted to be left behind, so she always ran as fast as she could to keep up with Angel.

Together, they sniffed out new and fascinating smells, they enjoyed endless belly rubs, and they snuggled each and every night. They were finally safe and loved, together forever in their happy forever home.

From left to right: Renie, Donna, Bobbie, Rita

About the Authors

Rita Gigante is a sought-out psychic medium, spiritual healer, and published author. Her memoir, *The Godfather's Daughter: An Unlikely Story of Love, Healing, and Redemption*, was published in 2012. Rita is co-owner of Space of Grace Healing with her wife Bobbie in Tappan, New York.
www.spaceofgracehealing.com

Bobbie Sterchele is a registered nurse, a gifted intuitive healer, energy worker, and psych-K practitioner. Bobbie is co-owner of Space of Grace Healing with her wife Rita in Tappan, New York.

Award-winning children's author Donna McDine writes from her home in Tappan, New York. McDine is a member of the SCBWI, NYS Reading Association, and Family Reading Partnership.
www.DonnaMcDine.com

About the Illustrator

Maureen "Renie" De Mase studied art in New York City and is a mixed medium freelance artist. Renie creates in her home studio in Ramsey, New Jersey, and is a proud owner of Renie's Art. Renie is also a member of the Graphic Artist Guild.
Instagram: @renies_art